BEST FRIENDS

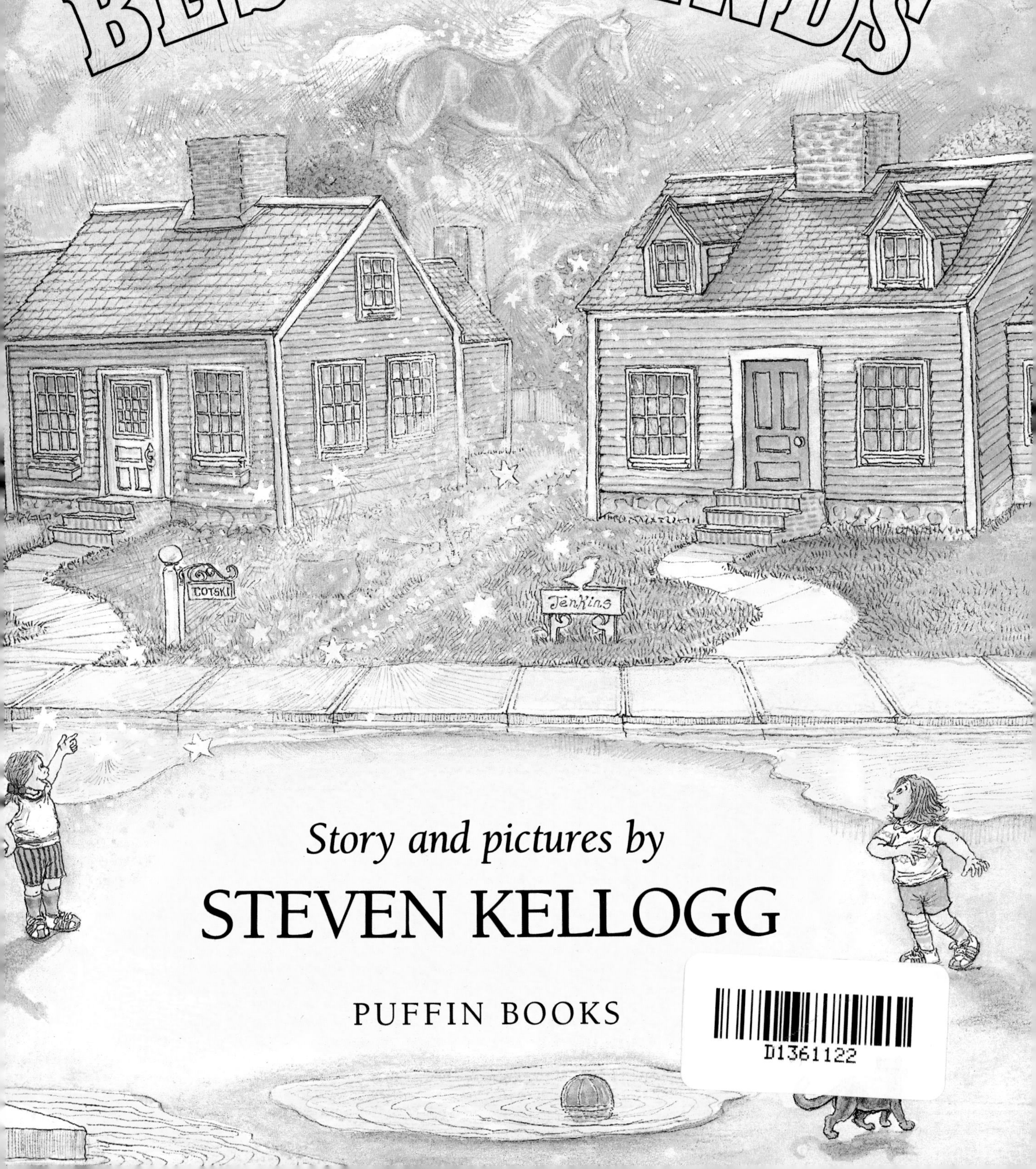

Story and pictures by

STEVEN KELLOGG

PUFFIN BOOKS

PUFFIN BOOKS
Published by the Penguin Group
Penguin Putnam Books for Young Readers, 345 Hudson Street,
New York, New York 10014, U.S.A.
Penguin Books Ltd, 27 Wrights Lane, London W8 5TZ, England
Penguin Books Australia Ltd, Ringwood, Victoria, Australia
Penguin Books Canada Ltd, 10 Alcorn Avenue, Toronto, Ontario, Canada M4V 3B2
Penguin Books (N.Z.) Ltd, 182-190 Wairau Road, Auckland 10, New Zealand
Penguin Books Ltd, Registered Offices: Harmondsworth, Middlesex, England

Library of Congress Catalog Card Number: 85-15971
Printed in the U.S.A.
First Pied Piper Printing 1990
E

39 37 38 40

A Pied Piper Book is a registered trademark of Dial Books for Young Readers,
a division of Penguin Books USA Inc.,
®™ 1,163,686 and ®™ 1,054,312.

BEST FRIENDS
is published in a hardcover edition by Dial Books for Young Readers.
ISBN 0-14-054607-3

The full-color artwork was prepared using ink and pencil line and watercolor washes.
It was then scanner-separated and reproduced as red, blue, yellow, and black halftones.

For Emily and Amy…with love

Louise Jenkins and I love horses, but we aren't allowed to have real ones.

I said, "Let's pretend that a stallion named Golden Silver-wind lives in a stable between our houses." Louise loved the idea.

At school we pushed our desks together.

And we played on the same team.

At lunch we shared our chocolate milk.

Chocolate is Louise's favorite, and it's mine too.

After school we pretended that we rode Golden Silverwind. Our magic witch hats gave us the power to make our neighborhood anything we wanted it to be.

And after dark, when it seemed to be haunted, we weren't scared as long as we were together.

We were best friends.

Summer came, and so did Louise's aunt and uncle. They took her to a mountain resort for a vacation. Louise told me that she didn't want to go. "It will be awful," she said. "And I'll miss you every day."

When she left, our neighborhood turned into a lonely desert.

If only Louise would be able to escape.

I even wished she'd get a contagious disease so they'd have to let her come home.

I wouldn't be afraid of catching it. I'd nurse her back to health with chocolate milk.

I missed her so much! I wished that Golden Silverwind and I could rescue her!

Finally I got a postcard. It said:

Dear Kathy,

This place is terrific. Yesterday I saw three deer behind the lodge. There are lots of kids my age, and Aunt Pat and Uncle Bart take us camping on Pine Cone Peak. I hope you're having fun too.

Love from your friend,
Louise

Later I heard Mrs. Jenkins say that Louise had made lots of new friends and was having the best summer of her life.

It wasn't fair. She wasn't lonely like me. She wasn't missing me at all.

Louise Jenkins was a traitor! She was my *worst* friend.

I wished that a volcanic eruption would blast Pine Cone Peak into pebbles.

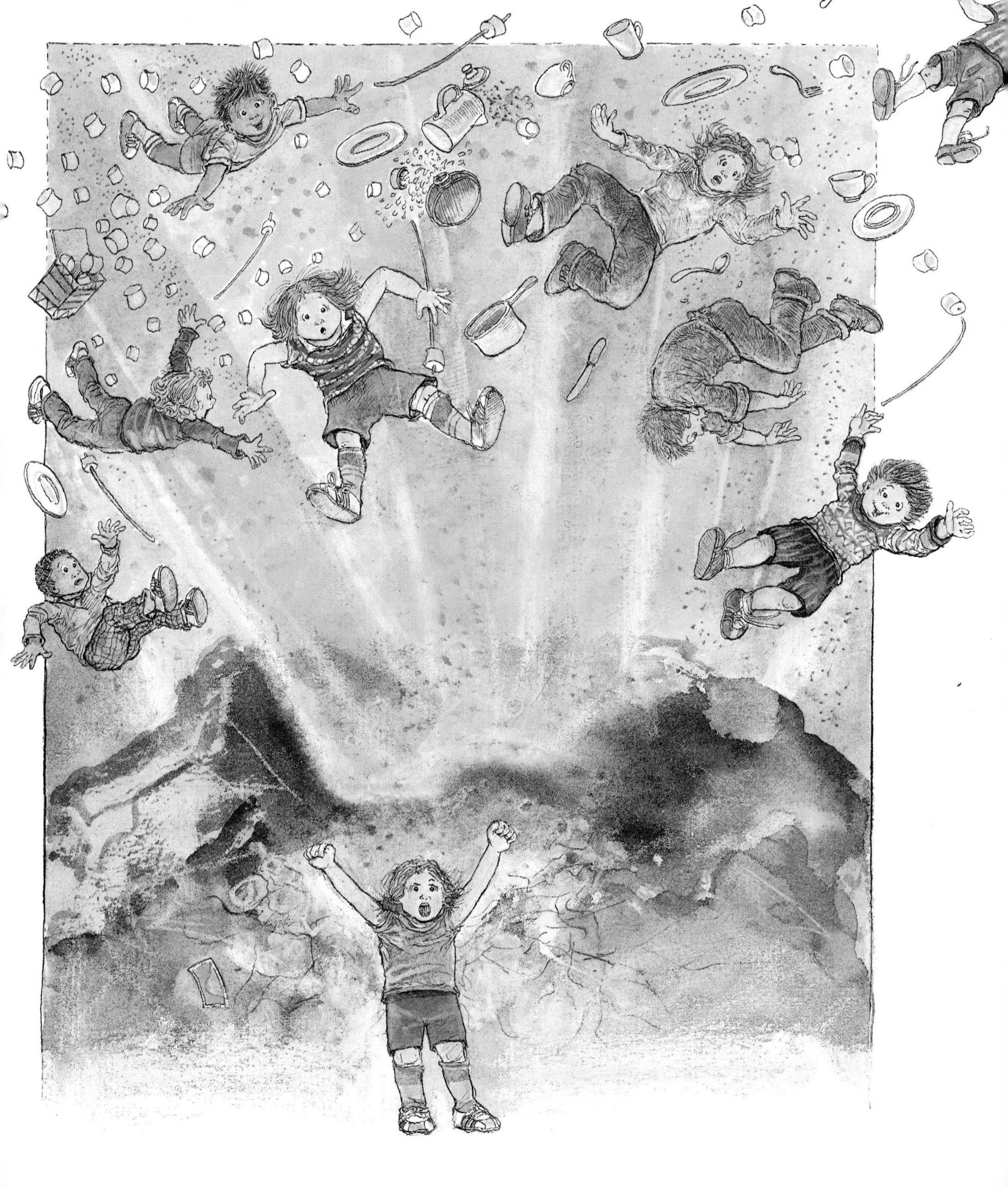

Mom told me not to be jealous of Louise's new friends.

Later she said, "I heard that the house across the street has been sold. Maybe there'll be someone your age in the new family."

I prayed for fifty kids my age. Fifty new best friends with *real* horses!

When the moving man came, I asked him, "How many people in the new family?"

He said, "One."

I asked if it was someone my age.

He said, "Nope, it's Mr. Jode. He's seventy-two."

This was the worst summer of my life! The new family was one old man!

Mom said we should be good neighbors, and she sent me to invite Mr. Jode for a cookout.

When he saw my witch hat he said, "I wish you'd use your magic powers to help me find good homes for the new puppies that Sarah is expecting."

I ran home to ask Mom if I could have one. She said yes.

I couldn't wait to have a puppy of my own. And if Louise Jenkins wanted to play with it after she got back from Pine Cone Peak I'd say "NEVER!" That would fix her.

Mr. Jode and I talked about how much fun it would be when the puppies were born. I told him I wanted a spotted one just like Sarah.

"The first spotted one will be yours," he promised.

One day Mrs. Jenkins showed up and said, "I understand that your dog is expecting puppies. I'd like to reserve one for my daughter, Louise."

I couldn't stand to think of Louise having one of Sarah's puppies. I told Mr. Jode that I would keep all of them.

Mr. Jode said, "Three years ago Sarah had eight puppies in one litter. Would your mother want that many dogs?"

I had to admit that eight dogs would drive my mom crazy.

Mr. Jode asked me if I was afraid that Louise wouldn't give her puppy a good home.

I had to admit that she would.

A week later Louise came back. Her mother had already told her that we were both getting puppies, and she was all excited about us raising them together.

Next she started talking about all the campouts on Pine Cone Peak, and how her uncle and aunt had already planned a return trip for the following summer.

I pretended to be very interested in my book.

Then she told me that she was glad to be home, and that she had missed me very much.

She had brought me a red Pine Cone Peak sweatshirt, a sparrow's feather, a rock collection, and a whistle on a lanyard that she had woven herself.

I told her how much I'd missed her. But I didn't tell her how mad I had been.

I took Louise to meet my new friends. I knew that they would all like each other, and they did. I said, "Aren't Sarah's spots beautiful? I'm going to get the first puppy that looks like her."

A few nights later Mr. Jode called to say that Sarah was having her puppies.

By the time we arrived, one puppy had already been born. It was brown. Mr. Jode handed him to Louise saying, "When he grows up, he'll look just like Sarah's mother."

Sarah went to sleep. Mr. Jode and Louise made hot chocolate and tried to think of a name for her puppy. I couldn't wait for mine to be born.

Sarah slept for hours. Finally Mr. Jode said, "It looks like there's only one puppy this time. Sarah has never had such a small litter before."

I felt awful.

It wasn't fair! Louise got to spend the whole summer camping on Pine Cone Peak, and now she had Sarah's only puppy.

Louise said, "I think the brown puppy should belong to both of us. We could name him Golden Silverwind."

Mr. Jode said, “I’ll build him a dog house between your houses.”

“And Sarah and I will help with his training.”

When I got home, I kept thinking how lucky I was to have a special friend like Louise. I was already worried about how much I would miss her when she went away next summer.

But at least this time when she's camping on Pine Cone Peak I'll have Golden Silverwind all to myself.